Up an

MW01225917

written by Pam Holden
illustrated by Kelvin Hawley

1

Helicopters go up
and down.

Escalators go up
and down.

Yo-yos go up
and down.

Kites go up
and down.

9

Dolphins go up
and down.

See-saws go up
and down.

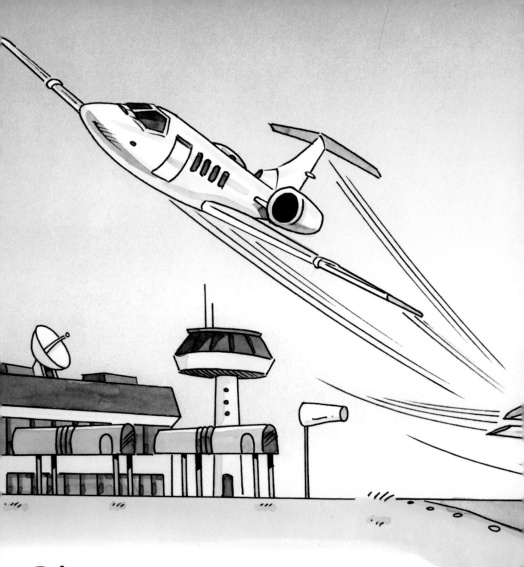

Planes go up
and down.

Swings go up
and down, too.